The Kitchen Fairy

Tam e. Polzer

Louise,

I'm so glad to share this world with you. Shine on and keep on smiling.

♡ Jam e.

ISBN: ISBN-10: **1511526521**
ISBN-13: ISBN-13: **978-1511526524**

DEDICATION

I dedicate this book to my parents, Betty Lou and William Lewis Walrath. Although they are no longer living on this Earth, I know the lessons they instilled in me, their love for me and others, and their passion for life will be carried on by the Kitchen Fairies and Guardian Angels who are still guiding and making life better for those they love.

CONTENTS

ACKNOWLEDGMENTS

I would like to thank Gretchen Reed for being my mentor, editor and dear friend; Margie DeLong, author of the beautifully written book, *Grand Observations: A Year of Weekly Visits to the Grand River at the Blair Road Bridge*, for encouraging me to publish on Create Space and for organizing Words and Wine (an inspiring local poetry reading series held at "Your Vine or Mine?" in Painesville, Ohio); M. E. Betsy McMillan, author of the inspiring and lovely book, *A Mystery in the Mailbox*, for conducting a very informative writing group called "Water's Edge" held in Kirtland, Ohio, and for helping me with my back cover and many details; my niece, Cheri, for taking photos of my initial front and back cover, my niece, Lori, for some final editing; my daughter, Eva, for giving me the idea for and guidance during the creation of my cover; my mother-in-law, Ruth, for her helpful comments and for letting me use her refrigerator over and over again for experimenting with and designing my cover (not many people have a refrigerator with a handle on the right side); my son, Lou, for his constant encouragement with my writing; and my husband, Bob, for his honesty.

Part One: L.o.v.e. Notes

Dad wanted boys, and I guess just having me, a girl, didn't cut it. So, after seven years of no luck, one night of God's touch and eight months of too much, L.O.V.E. came into our house. Although Lilly was the last to be born, she stood for the first letter in L.O.V.E. She was one in a quadruplet. Owen, Violet and Ellis completed the four-letter word. With L.O.V.E. came chaos, creating craziness in my once calm family. Dad freaked out daily, Mom hit bottom, and as the old saying goes, the you-know-what hit the fan for us kids. Thank God for the Kitchen Fairy.

"What is all this crumbumble?" yelled Dad as he stepped on the blocks beneath the pile of unmatched socks. Then he stepped on Violet's robotic dinosaur. It probably wouldn't have been that bad, but when he landed, his knee crammed into one of Ellis's matchbox cars. But that wasn't the worst of it. The wing of an airplane pierced the palm of his hand, and the plastic green monkey half in its barrel actually stuck up his nostril. When Lilly started laughing, Dad yowled. Then he threw things. Cars skidded in all directions. Socks sailed down into the basement. Blocks bounced off the ceiling. Owen's dirty underwear stuck to the ceiling fan. See what I mean about the you-know-what hitting the fan?

Ellis tried to escape it all--kept fiddling with the key in the lock of the door Dad called "forbidden." When Dad saw that Ellis had the key, he actually dove toward Ellis, grabbed and threw the key across the room, yelling loudly and clearly that the door went nowhere and was not to be tampered with. Then Dad stepped backward into sacks still packed with groceries. Fresh strawberries and grapes squashed. Boxes of cereal and noodles crushed. Jars of pickles and applesauce shattered when he threw them out the back door. "Why aren't things where they belong?" he screamed. I tried to imagine a 3-D painting of flowers in a meadow, but all I could think about was that I should have put the groceries away.

I would have, too, but "Life happened," as Mom always said. I can't quite remember what else happened on that particular day with Dad, but I distinctly remember what happened another day after I had just brought in the last bag. Lilly's screams crescendoed and Ellis started yelling, "Mom, come quick, ya gotta come quick. Violet's climbing onto the roof with her bare feet, and Owen is hanging from a wire over the road!" I can understand why Mom left the burner on.

I understood a lot of things Mom did. I helped her with the mountains of laundry, the ungracious grocering, the constant cooking and cleaning. If it wasn't the spaghetti-stained t-shirt stuck to the stereo or the butter wiped on Dad's boat shoes, it was squashed bananas and pulled-up plants and dirt spread on the carpet like cinnamon on toast. If it wasn't every item of clothing from two dressers tossed into the air for fun, it was peed on sheets, toothpaste spit on the mirror or poop smeared on the toilet seat.

Dad didn't get it, though. He'd been lost in another dimension. I didn't find out until years later why he had changed so much. I just blamed it on L.O.V.E. He just couldn't handle the chaos they caused, and he didn't see Mom's non-stop, chopped-up actions, the one hundred small accomplishments, the robotic hum-drum she dealt with daily. He was too busy working twelve hours a day, and when he came home to clutter and a woman too tired to tend to him as she used to, he lost his temper. Frustrated, he'd ask Mom, "Why is the house like this? What do you do all day?" and of course she'd say, "Eat bonbons and watch soaps, what do you think?" I seriously think he believed her, because one day he said, "I can't believe you let the children take over the house while you sit on the couch like a potato." I thought, *Really, Dad? The only way Mom is like a potato is that she has eyes in the back of her head.* And I swear she had extra arms. She could fold five baskets of laundry, prepare, serve and put away three meals and two snacks, wipe noses, spills and rear ends all day long, and the woman still had enough compassion and patience to help with puzzles and pick up parts.

Most importantly, Mom could mend anything from broken hearts to the crack of dawn as if that was her purpose from the start. One day, though, she took a little extra time on songs, and Ellis finally made it through the alphabet with writing only one letter wrong. That's the day Dad told Mom we lived like pigs. He told Mom she *was* a pig and he couldn't stand the fact that his children would be pigs, too.

That's the same night the Kitchen Fairy came to our house for the first time. When I woke up and walked into the kitchen to put on the coffee, I could see the burnt orange color of the kitchen counter for the first time in three years. No bills, spare change, keys, balls, battleships, or clippings of coupons cluttered the countertop. On the floor I saw white tiles that I forgot existed. I was so used to seeing the braided rugs there that Great Grandma made. Mom said they helped insulate, and Mom was our insulator.

I watched Dad's eyes grow large as he absorbed the naked kitchen. The acorn collection on the countertop was gone. The weeds and the green bean can they were growing in--gone. The dead butterfly on a butter dish--gone. All the magnets and photos on the fridge were gone. The newest chore list had disappeared. My latest drawing of geese in flight must have flown away. All the dishes piled high in the sink had sunk out of sight, and the cow cookie jar filled with farm animals must have been corralled during the night. The toaster, the can opener, the coffee can, and the tin cans covered with crayon creations sitting in every crevice of the kitchen were canned from the counter. No kidding! Even the crinkled v-like lines that I thought were permanently engrained in Dad's forehead disappeared.

Only two things sat on the kitchen counter. One was Dad's coffee "mug" he had made of Mom in college (out of clay he had molded a coffee cup having her face on it). The other was a note written on a green sticky note. (Green was dad's favorite color). It read:

To find peace, be still
and don't forget to breathe.
Remember that you have a choice:
Attitude is everything.

--Love and hugs, The Kitchen Fairy

Dad tilted his head to the side, having a quizzical look on his face, and then seeming to reach an understanding, he breathed in deeply, as if smelling roses, and then he smiled and let out a sigh as if admiring an angel.

And I did see an angel, I swear, flutter past the kitchen window. Dad must have seen or felt her presence, too, because he did something really weird. He walked over to the window and whispered, "Thank you, my angel." Then he kissed the stained glass heart hanging there that he made, or was it the angel now invisible to me that he kissed? I still don't know for sure.

Actually, at the time, I didn't know anything for sure. But neither did anyone else. We used to have brains, but somehow they disappeared in what Mom called "Baby Limbo." Before L.O.V.E., we not only had brains, but we had peace, order, flow--we sailed a pretty boring river. After L.O.V.E., we rode the rapids, barely holding onto our raft.

Dad rarely could keep hold of his grip, and he bailed out often. He needed order, so when he heard Mom's sweet voice begin to sing in the morning, he jumped overboard, left for work before L.O.V.E. woke up, hoping to escape before the white water rushed. Like I said, he needed a smooth ride, and living with quads was like swirling in a whirlpool.

Although L.O.V.E. shared the same womb, that didn't mean they got along together in the same room. One day just after Dad left I could hear Lilly ordering everybody around. "Owen, don't splash water on the floor, and you should tell Mom to pick those potatoes out of your ears. Eewwee. Ellis, take off my bear slippers and blow your booger nose—it's gross. Violet, you're pouring in too many bubbles and you better wipe off that picture on the wall you drew with Mom's eye stuff. Owen, you ovbiously (She was articulate but couldn't pronounce everything correctly) don't care that much about your army guys since they're not back in their bag." Then she'd proceeded to throw them in the box that would be tossed in the garbage if not put away by the next day. Believe me, this caused a lot of crying and wrestling-on-the-floor battles. And she was a perfectionist, like Dad. Her surroundings always looked like a museum. She arranged her animals on her bed according to height, her dolls according to age, her beads, clothes and hair ribbons according to kind and color. She drove us all nuts because she was always so dramatic if everything wasn't perfect. "My head is going to blow off," she'd say, or "I think I might die!" Poor little thing. If one speck of dirt or food stained her clothes, she changed. Mom said she went through more clothes than all of us put together. She was a tremendous help to Mom, though, like a little mother, when she wanted to be, when she wasn't feeling like a victim of one circumstance or another, but if someone spilled milk, she'd yank on her hair and scream, as if the spilled milk actually hurt her, but then she'd run for the rag and wipe up the mess. If anybody had hair out of place or dirt on his face, she was combing hair and licking her thumb to rub. That's why the others were either running away from or tiptoeing around her, not wanting to make waves, you know, just how we all tried to act around Dad. But it was so hard not to make waves with quadruple winds.

The morning after Lilly flipped out at dinner because the cheese hadn't melted evenly on her tuna noodle and Ellis accidently dropped his plate and a gob of casserole plopped on her pants and splatted on the floor, making her certain she would die, the Kitchen Fairy left a pink sticky note attached to her favorite hair ribbon:

Seeking perfection is an awesome goal,
but don't let it drive you nuts.
Focusing on you and what you can control
takes courage and a lot of guts.

--Love and hugs, The Kitchen Fairy

While reading, Dad shook his head up and down and said to himself, it seemed, although he faced Lilly, "Yep. Get a grip. Don't flip out over stupid stuff." And, he added, "Use your brain."

Owen did. Use his brain, that is. At least his creative, right side. We called him "The King of Pretend," because every day he was something or someone different—a dog, a detective, a cartoon character. Once he wrapped his hands and feet in double faced tape and ran around pressing them against trees, hoping he would stick, saying he was a tree frog. Another time he jumped from the second story deck into a huge pile of snow, pretending to be a paratrooper. And the time he pretended to be a monkey escaping from a zoo was quite memorable. Sure, Owen used his brain, but I don't think it's the way Dad meant, because he acted before he thought. As I said earlier, Mom didn't turn off the burner one day when "life happened." That's the night we didn't have any supper because it all burned up. Actually, so did a corner of our kitchen. L.O.V.E. was supposed to be washing up for dinner, but Owen's imagination got the best of him, having just watched a documentary on monkeys on The Discovery Channel. He decided to be a run-away monkey and climbed out through his bedroom window onto the roof, convincing Violet to pick an animal to be as well and join him. He had tied Lilly's baby doll to his waist with a belt, because he was a mommy monkey, and he grabbed the telephone wire a tad above the roof and climbed out on it, a little way from the house, without thinking, of course, and hung from his knees, upside-down. Violet decided to be some tropical bird from the jungle, a bird with brains, a bird that stayed inside because it liked a warmer climate. Lilly must have decided to be a blue jay because she kept squawking--she wanted her doll back. That's when Ellis came running downstairs babbling that Mom had to come quick, so, distracted, she left supper on the stove with the burner on.

We were amazed how fast the firemen came. Especially since we didn't call them. Boy, did they come in handy when the kitchen caught on fire. They put out the fire in two minutes flat, but it took them ten minutes to convince Owen off of the phone line. "The 'perry chicker' isn't red like it's supposed to be" or "Monkeys hang with their babies all day long" or "That fireman doesn't look like the one in my coloring book" were all excuses that kept him air-bound. Lilly finally convinced him to jump into the yellow cherry picker by saying, "Your friends miss you at the zoo." And Ellis said he would make his bed for a week if he would come down immediately. Finally, Owen came down, but boy was he angry that everybody interrupted his cool game. The next day the Kitchen Fairy left a blue note, tucked inside Owen's Fire engine.

Playing is fun and good
and pretending at times is fine
as long as you don't hurt others
or put your life on the line.

--Love and hugs, The Kitchen Fairy

Dad said, "For God's sake, mind your mother, be real, and use your brain."

Violet seemed to use her brain to beautify herself and her surroundings. One time she snuck into Mom's make-up and painted pink pansies on the bedroom wall with new lipstick. Another time she made a huge rainbow on the kitchen door with permanent markers. And she always made the most unique creations. While she ate, she'd create beautiful designs with her food. Once she made a green bean house with bread as the door and windows, lettuce leaves as the roof, and corn kernels as the daffodils. She sprayed it with hairspray and left it on the kitchen counter to dry. We called her the recycler, because she could turn anything ready to be tossed away into usable, workable things. Of course the box for Dad's new table saw became her fort, well, everyone's fort. Acorns became a family of people. Dad's scrap wood became fences for Lilly's animals, hide-outs or airplanes for Owen's army guys, doctor supplies or dishes for Ellis's hospital or restaurant. Egg cartons worked well for baby doll sinks, couches or coffee tables. She also carried around a notebook and drew sketches of everyone she saw. Everything she made she believed to be beautiful whether it be a mud pie, a bubble beard or a catsup drawing.

I thought Dad was going to brain her the day she decided to "complete" his plans for the barn he designed. The plans, printed out, lay on his drafting table—he was old school. Earlier in the week I had seen Dad pointing out to her where the stalls would be for each animal and where the hay loft would be.

Violet wanted to surprise him and fill the barn with animals, so she piled broken-up spaghetti noodles for hay in the loft, put dabs of Cool Whip on marshmallows for sheep, squirts of mustard for chickens, Tootsie Rolls for horses and strips of sausage for the pigs. She even put down raisins for the you-know-what. Actually, she created quite a picture, believing it to be her best art ever.

And she made everyone laugh, except Dad. Too bad he had a meeting with the architect five minutes after he found her creative drawing. He was so angry he threw the drawing up in the air and it caught in the fan, whipping her condiment collection on the walls. (See, I told you the you-know-what hit the fan more than once for us kids). Then Dad told Violet to go to her room for the rest of the evening and think about what she had done.

Violet found a rainbow sticky note on her art easel in the morning.

When on your search
for beauty
in this world
so true,
remember to look
within us all,
especially
inside you.

--Love and hugs, The Kitchen Fairy

By the next day, Dad had calmed down, but he still stared at her with his serious Dad face and said, "Don't make a mess for your mother and don't touch other people's stuff. Use your brain!"

Ellis used his brain to serve everyone else. He was our kind, honest, protective kid. Mom called him her "informer." She never had to ask, "Hey, what's going on?" because Ellis would be puffing and blurting things out before she had a chance to ask questions. "Violet's making sand castles with your favorite tea cups," or "Owen's on the roof again--this time with an umbrella. He says he wants to fly like Mary Poppins," Or "Lilly's wearing *my* clean turtle shirt because Owen wiped his booger on hers." Mom always knew he told the honest truth, because he never thought to lie. In fact, he'd blush playing pretend with Owen. Even though all the kids called him "tattle tale," everybody liked him because he was disgustingly nice, a servant at everyone's fingertips. He'd do our jobs for us if we asked, and even when we didn't. And I never heard him say anything to be mean. He simply stated facts. "Owen, your breath smells like the elephants' cage," or, "Dad, your beard grows in patches like our lawn," or "Mom, that black hair growing out of your chin is getting long enough to be a leash."

One time Ellis pretty darn near saved Owen's life. Owen was pretending to be a blind chicken crossing the road, so he didn't see the bicyclist coming. Ellis yelled, pushing Owen out of the way, nearly being hit himself. When Owen fell to the side of the road on his face and saw the bicyclist swoop around to see if everyone was Okay, he realized what had happened. "Wow! You saved me! You are the best brother, Ellis. You're my super hero!" Ellis blushed, saying "No. No. I'm just a simple servant." When Owen heard that, he took it to the hilt, pretending that Ellis was his "simple-servant-super hero." All week long Ellis catered to his brother, even more than usual, bringing him his pillow, blanket, toys, and cleaning up his side of the room, taking his dirty clothes downstairs, and being the simple-servant-super hero that Owen wanted him to be. At the end of the week the Kitchen Fairy left a white sticky note on Ellis's medical bag that said the following:

It's Okay to wait on,
but don't be walked on.
Make your limits; be brave.
Be a warrior, not a slave!

--Love and hugs, The Kitchen Fairy

Dad shook his head in agreement on this one. "People take advantage if you're too nice," he mumbled, and of course he added, "Use your brain."

As you can tell, the Kitchen Fairy left all kind of notes. Each morning Dad found one in a clean section of the house--on a mirror, under a pillow, in a drawer. I stuck them all to the side of the fridge, to be good reminders for us. In fact, I still keep two of my favorites on my own fridge today.

I remember when Dad and I found one of my two favorites the night after I heard him and Mom talking about who they were B. C. (before children). I guess I never thought about who they were before they were parents. I didn't mean to eavesdrop, I swear, but my bedroom was right beneath theirs, and their voices could be heard through the laundry shoot as clearly as I saw that angel's blue eyes.

"I'm not some peon who fixes toilets, shovels snow and builds cabinets in a shoebox shop that has crap for tools. I can't believe this hillbilly operation I work for makes millions. I miss having my own business, building my own furniture. I don't know how much longer I can lower my standards for the productivity of someone else. If I hear 'This isn't a church,' or 'Close enough,' one more time, I'm going to throw-up."

"I know it's hard for you to work for someone else. With all of your artistic talent you must feel like a bird with clipped wings in a glass room. You see freedom but can't have it," answered Mom.

"Yeah, I'm trapped in someone else's shop for the sake of making money. The sad thing is, I never see a dime of it."

"Believe me, Dear. I understand."

"How can you possibly understand? You're home doing what you want whenever you want."

"Excuse me?"

"You're not being torn a million ways."

"What? You obviously don't have a clue. I had a life before children, too, you know. I've had to make sacrifices, too, you know. At least you can see something concrete at the end of your day and say 'I built that.' I work my butt off all day long and nobody knows. We've both given up a lot for children, but we didn't want Hope to be an only child, remember? We can't forget what we went through to get not one more, but four more. We can't forget to be thankful for what we have. I'm tired, but I'm thankful."

"I wasn't expecting quads."

"No person in his right mind would expect quads, but we have what we have and they are our priority now. We have to put our other life on hold and let some things go. I've let go of sleep, and I've let go of keeping a perfect house, and I've let go of my paying job. You've let go of working for yourself so we can have medical benefits. I know it's hard right now, but it won't be like this forever. We have to learn to enjoy this life--right now. They won't be young forever, and we can deal with this if we triple team them. Hope helps so much and is so good.

"Maybe you two can deal with this, but I can't. It's different with girls and women. They can deal with children. And you—well, you can deal with anything."

"I'm not dealing as well as you think."

"From working in the emergency room, you were used to dealing with confusion. You've even admitted that you thrived on it. And you experienced all types of people. You understand people. I was used to working alone, building all day in the basement at my own pace and then enjoying a peaceful household with just us and Hope. Now I have to deal with stupid people at work who just want to slap things together-- I'm so embarrassed that I can't even put my name on things anymore. Everybody's in a hurry and nobody cares about craftsmanship anymore."

"I appreciate your craftsmanship."

"Well, you don't count."

"Obviously."

"And after working with idiots all day I come home to a chaotic madhouse. I love them, Faith, but I feel like I'm losing it. I miss you. Are we ever going to have time to be together, like before?"

"Yes. Have faith."

"Really? Have faith? After all that's happened, I don't have faith anymore. And I don't even feel like I have you. And it seems like we're never gonna get caught up so I can do what I want to do again."

"Yes, we will."

"How can you be so positive?"

"We all have our health and we live in a beautiful home that you built. We have a lot to be thankful for. Our life isn't easy now, but I promised myself no matter how hard the balancing act was that I'd make time to show love for my family, play and pray with the kids. Time goes so fast. We'll never get these days back."

"I know, but I'm having a hard time enjoying these days because I keep questioning why things have happened as they have, and sometimes I wish it was just you and me and Hope again. Then I wouldn't be freaking out all the time. I can't stand the confusion and I can't stand the mess."

"Can't you just see beyond the crumbumble and take time to enjoy the little ones? You're always such a grouch. They don't know the man I fell in love with. I seriously think you should be treated for depression. You're either working, sleeping, yelling or feeling hopeless lately. There's help for you out there."

"I'm sorry. I thought by now that the kids would have filled the void, replaced the pain."

"Honey, you can't expect the kids to fill your void. You need to do that yourself by forgiving yourself and letting go of the past. The word 'forgive' literally means to let go, ya know? You need to let go so you can heal."

"I can't let go. And I really can't cope with the chaos. I'm losing it. I need order to think clearly, and there's never ever any order. At work I'm tripping over tools because nobody cares about efficiency and a clean work area, and then I come home and there's always too much crap lying around. I need to come home to a clean house. You need to hire a professional house cleaner."

"Okay. Let's do this. You seek a professional to help you with your depression, and I'll seek a professional to help with the house."

"I wish you could just teach them to pick up. Then we wouldn't have to spend the money."

"We pick up a hundred times a day. Do you think we just play all day long?"

"I don't know. I just wish there was a Kitchen Fairy in every room every day so I could have some sanity."

"Believe me, so do we. Now, go to sleep."

When Mom said 'we,' I'm not sure if she meant her and us kids or her and The Kitchen Fairy. Actually I thought she *was* the Kitchen Fairy which would all make sense. Trying to appease Dad, she'd stay up all night, make order and write her notes. But I didn't understand how the next two notes sort of came from nowhere. Let me explain.

The next morning I found Dad sitting in the middle of the foyer floor. Wow. I almost forgot it was maroon marble, because I was so used to seeing the mess from the daily tornado. But this morning, fire engines, balls, dolls, cars, stuffed bears, hares and vinyl bean bag chairs were gone. When the grandfather's clock chimed six times, I was mesmerized. I forgot about the beauty in its base, waist and face. In the forehead of the clock's face was a space showing stages of the moon, now in a quarter phase. The last time I really noticed the moon was full. The golden pendulum silently swayed back and forth in front of the uneven weights in the waist. Last time I remember the golden weights all lined up evenly. At the base, perfectly placed, a swirl slept within the grain of the wormy white ash wood. "Wow! I remember when I helped you make that clock, Dad. I forgot how awesome it is. You used to make a lot of things, didn't you?"

"When I had time."

"Mom always says that the only thing we really have is time.

"Yeah, but there's never enough to really do what I want right now."

"What do you really want?"

"Oh, it doesn't matter. I had it once, but I'll never have it again."

"Dad. You're an artist. You can create . . . anything."

Just then, a breeze blew through the window and a note fluttered down, it seemed from nowhere.

All we have is time right now
to live this very minute.
Yes, learn from the past
and plan for the future,
yet, for the Present, Live in It.

--Love and hugs, The Kitchen Fairy

I kind of melted into Dad then, because he gave me a huge hug and said, "Thanks." I don't know if he was talking to me or the Kitchen Fairy, but it felt really good. We hadn't hugged in years. That's why that letter still hangs on my fridge.

My favorite letter of all, though, found us--Dad, me and a bunch of strangers--at 4 a.m. a few days later. It happened like this.

While in my bed, at midnight, I heard the usual Kitchen Fairy noises--clattering dishes, running water, humming vacuum cleaner. At 3 a.m., I heard more of the usual noises when Dad worked a double shift--the twist, click and closing of the door. But then I heard a thud. My body jumped out of my bed. I ran out of my room and down the stairs to see what was happening. I saw Dad on his knees in the kitchen. Then I saw Mom's body. She looked like a rag doll thrown to the floor with her neck cramped too tightly against the kitchen cabinet, her body twisted unnaturally.

I trembled. Dad's mouth opened like a draw bridge, joining the scene to some sort of understanding in his mind. Then he yanked the cord out of the wall that she could have tripped over. He picked up the vacuum cleaner and heaved it into the French doors. Glass shattered like his emotions. After huddling to the floor, his body shook, he pounded his fist on the floor and he cried. All I could do was say, "God, help us now," as I sat crouched beneath the dining room table.

Then I swear everything seemed to slow way down, and I saw the angel in the window. Her light shined through, making the stained glass heart hanging there glow. And her blue eyes…Wow. When her blue eyes peered through the glass, they connected with mine and I remember feeling a soft, warm breeze as from the beating of her wings. Right then my soul filled up with peace. Somehow I knew things were gonna be Okay.

I didn't know if he saw her light, as I did. I didn't know if he felt the flutter of her wings as I did, but Dad must have heard the angel's words that I didn't, because I watched my father's storm stop and his following actions calmed my fears. The broken man transformed into his old, younger self, calm and steady. It's as if the angel slipped inside him, guided him. My father sat up, wiped his face with his sleeve and took a deep breath. He pulled Mom's head away from the cabinet, brought her limbs in close to her, close to him; next he checked her pulse. Then he swiped his finger in her mouth, tilted her head back and brought his lips to hers. Her chest expanded three times. Then he placed his hands on her chest and pressed firmly into her ribs. It seemed forever that I watched the mechanical routine, although in reality all this happened in just a few seconds. Puff, puff. Push, push, push, push. Puff, puff. Push, push, push . . . the whole scene didn't seem real. Mom's lifeless body, silent lips, white skin. I felt totally detached, like this wasn't really happening, like it was a play and I knew no actors in it.

But within a blink, everything changed. During a puff, life flowed back into my mother. Her face turned pale pink just after the paramedics walked through the broken French doors. Dad and I both leaped up from the simultaneous actions. Mom whispered, "Where's the light?" while the paramedics shouted, "Where's the woman?"

Everyone stared at one another before the next onslaught of questions fired.

"Are you Okay, Honey?"

"What happened to the light?"

"How did you make her breathe, Daddy?"

"How did you know to come?"

"Didn't someone dial 911?"

"Where did that light go"?

"What have I done to you?"

"Who is *she*?"

Everyone stared, this time at the angel. From the breeze of her wings the glass heart tapped the window in sync with my heart beat; then her face faded gently into the night, like the sound of faraway train whistle. An unsigned note from above fluttered down like a butterfly into our view and in big, bold letters read:

How deep is your faith?

Stunned, everyone seemed to answer internally. One stared, someone shook his head side to side, another nodded. I still felt that warm presence within me. Dad squeezed my hand and kissed Mom's cheek. Mom said softly, "I want to find that light again." Then she closed her eyes. A strange way to go looking for the light.

Tam e. Polzer

Part Two: Words of Faith

Well, when Dad went to the hospital, I was left
alone in charge until Aunt Cindy could get off work.
A lot happened, too. Lilly, as you may remember, was
a lot like Dad. If routine changed or things didn't go
as planned, she had a hard time jumping the hurdle to
move on. She freaked--it was pretty bad--and became
out-of-control mad. "Where is Mother? I want my
mother!" she kept screaming, even after I told her she
wasn't here. She didn't like my answer, and running
around the room like a taunted caged animal, she spun
and fell, hands first, on Owen's night-time pull-up
that he'd forgotten to throw in the trash. Trying to
make light of the matter, embarrassed, Owen said,
"Let's pretend this pull-up is a lost alien and we have
to help it go home." He flung the pull-up into the air.
There it was again: the you-know-what hitting the fan.
The diaper broke the ceiling light and then flung from
the fan. White goop splattered all over the room, and
glass shattered down like a hail storm.

Eight eyes looked at me for direction. "Freeze!" I
blurted out, surprising myself with such assertiveness.
I used to be such a quiet one, acquiescing to all, not
feeling my opinion mattered, but enough of that, I

thought. "Nobody move!" Of course Owen didn't listen. He ran out of the room, stepped on some glass and cut his heel. Lilly cried out, "He's bleeding on my carpet!" Violet mouthed, "Wow! Wow!" Ellis brought us back to reality. "I'm gonna tell Mom. Mommy!" We all stood in silence, then, staring, waiting. This was the first time Mom didn't come when we really needed her. We were at a loss. But you know what? She still didn't let us down, because just then, we all saw her. The angel, I mean. Mom sent her, I'm sure. The angel didn't say a word, but her wings dried our tears and her light eased our fears. Her peace filled the room with warmth like a sunrise would light the horizon. Then she faded into the room's blue walls.

Silently, Lilly pulled out the shop vac; Ellis, the sliver of glass in Owen's foot; Violet, our clothes. Nobody said a word. Which was weird. What was weirder, though, was before eating breakfast, we all held hands and prayed in unison a verse Mom used to say at bedtime and one that the Kitchen Fairy knew as well.

> "When we believe that All is One,
> honor thyself and honor everyone,
> seek only the truth, know love is divine
> and live in the present time,
> we will all be fine."

Other than that, it was the quietest day I remember--until Dad came home, that is. Then we all talked at once.

"When is Mommy coming home?"

"Violet broke the glass."

"Owen got blood on the carpet."

"We ate cake for breakfast."

"We watched cartoons all day."

"Hope helped us make a blanket fort with the card table."

"Aunt Cindy brought us stew."

"We saw an angel."

Dad studied Violet's face. I knew she was thinking that he wouldn't believe her, but he pulled her close, said we should pray. What a day! I couldn't believe it. Dad never prayed with the quads before.

"Aren't you gonna kneel with us?" "Mommy always kneels with us to pray."

"No, she doesn't. Mom says we can pray, anytime, anywhere, anyway."

"Put your hands together, Daddy."

"Tell us what you're thankful for, Daddy. We always do that with Mommy."

"We do that one at the supper table."

"Let's do the angel of God one."

"No. That's the bedtime one. We don't even have our jammies on yet."

"How come you're crying, Daddy?"

Dad couldn't take it. He squeezed his face with his hands, hiding his tears, and then he yelled, "Pick up all of your toys and go to bed." That did *not* go over too well.

"I want Mommy back!"

"It's not bedtime yet. The little hand is not on the snowman!"

"We didn't pick out our favorite books!"

"I'm hungry!"

"Just listen to Dad. He's had a bad day!"

"Dad always has a bad day."

"Just go to bed!"

Wow. We cleared out like scared birds.

The next day, I didn't go to school till noon and Dad didn't go to work at all. He slept all day. At first, I tried to keep the children away from him, but after 9 o'clock I said, "Go ahead and try to wake up Daddy." Lilly lined up all of her stuffed animals around him, Violet drew a heart on his forehead with shaving cream, Ellis brought him a cup of coffee that I made him and Owen pretended that he was a zoologist giving a black bear a check-up. He didn't have to pretend much because Dad jumped up and screamed some of his incoherent-to-everyone-but-us language. "Whoda, whatda whenda, whereda?" Then he said if kids disturbed him one more time he'd stuff socks in their mouths and lock them in a closet.

I was pretty scared when I snuck up at 11 o'clock to tell him he had to call in the school to excuse my absence. "Why aren't you where you belong? You go to school this minute!" he screamed. I was so scared that I went, although I knew the children shouldn't be left alone while he slept. Fortunately it was just a few blocks away and I could walk. Before I left I called my aunt and the neighbor, but nobody was home. I don't think they knew what shape Dad was in or they would have made arrangements to be there for us. At school I told my counselor I needed to leave and help my Dad, so she called Aunt Cindy at work who made arrangements to meet me at home.

Dad was still zonked out when I arrived. Owen was pretending he was lost, searching for his parents in a blizzard, pulling around his wagon filled with blankets. Lilly, in the kitchen, was throwing out all the bowls that didn't have lids; Violet was in Mom and Dad's bathroom painting her toes five different colors; Ellis was sitting at the end of Dad's bed, rubbing Dad's feet like Mom used to do. He said, "I miss Mommy, and I want a new dad."

I didn't want a new dad. I just wanted my old one back. Even though I thought he always wanted boys before the quads, he still kind of liked me back then. I mean I was his gofer in the basement and he was always so appreciative. I felt glad to be his extra hand. And he bought me overalls like his and work boots and a hat. He even bought me my own tool set, a real one, and said every carpenter had to have the right tools. I was sad, too, that L.O.V.E. never knew the man I did. They never played "The Funny Bunny From Outer Space" with the plastic rabbit or "Dingle-do-dop" under the blankets in Mom and Dad's bed or "Down the Hatch" with the stacked pillows on the couch or "Froggy-Froggy" in the bathtub. They never played the game we made at dinner one night with Mom called "Monkey, Billy-goat, Reindeer, Chicken, Ahhhhh!" They didn't know how creative he was, how crazy he was, how funny he was.

They didn't know of his endless energy. They didn't know how he labored with such love while building them each a cradle, an awesome swing set and a horse carousel. I remember watching him build the horses, and I even helped paint them. Weird thing though, I never saw them again after Grandpa passed away. He died the day the quads were born and that was the end of my helping Dad in the basement. The only man they knew was working, sleeping or yelling because things weren't where they belonged.

L.O.V.E. sent him over the edge with just the simple details that Mom handled without a thought. The minute that any disturbance occurred--a battle or tattle or blanket fight, or somebody cried, not tucked in right--Dad yelled at the top of his lungs, went down to the basement or left the house.

Well, at this point, Dad had no choice. Mom had a serious concussion and had to stay in the hospital for another few days at least for observation. So, somebody had to take care of the details, details Mom called "Naptime Dilemmas," "Dinner Delight," "The Laundry Mountain," and the "Grocery Flight" to name a few. He sure had a different way to deal with details than Mom's patient, yet sufficient and successful time-outs and taking-away favorite-toys technique.

Dad dealt with things the only way he knew how…by following through with his threats. Let me tell you some examples.

Naptime dilemmas:

"I can't sleep with Violet's loud breathing!"

"Please read one more book!"

"Owen keeps snorting at me!"

"Believe me . . . I am not tired!"

"If you don't take a nap, you will have no supper and stay in your room the rest of the day!" Well, Owen, of course had to give one more snort, because after all he was pretending to be a pig, so he spent the rest of the day in his room.

Dinner delight:

"Look! Violet's swirling broccoli in her ketchup and drawing on the floor!"

"Owen's connecting straws and drinking out of Violet's cup from across the table."

"Lilly, can't you make it through one dinner without changing your clothes?"

"Dad! Ellis just snarfed his chocolate milk."

"That's it! Everyone to bed this minute!" It's hard to go to bed at 5 p.m., but we did.

The laundry mountain:

"I don't sniff clothes," so if you want them washed, bring them in your basket downstairs." (Dad thought he was coming up with something new). Since he could only do one thing at a time, you know, he did laundry all day. He actually smiled after we all helped him fold the last basket and take it upstairs. The problem was that when the kids took off all their clothes for the night, another mountain stood, tall enough for Owen to jump into it off of the washer without receiving injuries. Dad's eyes grew five times their size. He found a huge lawn bag and threw all of the clothes in it and tossed it into the garbage. So much for Lilly's favorite alligator shirt, Owen's Batman costume, Violet's art supplies in her pockets, Ellis's chef hat and Dad's wallet in his own pair of pants. Good thing I took the bag out of the garbage bin outside, because we needed Dad's wallet for our grocery experience.

The grocery flight:

We all went with Dad to the grocery store. He took with him one hundred dollars. That's what he used to give Mom to work with for the week. "One hundred dollars is one hundred dollars." He only said it once. "If you put something into the cart that I didn't ask for, I'm not going to have enough money and if I find that out at the register, I will be very embarrassed and we'll leave the store without buying a thing." Boy was he horrified when the cashier rang out $146.56. Dad kept his promise of leaving the store since somebody put stuff into the cart without his permission. But first he made the kids put everything back (against the cashier's wishes). I saw the store's manager look at Violet with pity when he heard her explanation to Dad about the solid brass candlesticks and pink candles. "Mommy told me a candle-light dinner with you was on her list, so I thought you could surprise her when she came home from the hospital." The manager's expression changed when Violet accidently knocked over the candle display. Clanging brass reverberated throughout the store and everyone's eyes found Dad. While Dad walked with Lilly to put back the bubble bath, I walked with Owen back to the meat department. The butcher scratched his head when he watched Owen put the meat back, hearing Owen tell me that he just wanted to surprise Dad with a big, juicy steak. Ellis, being the loving thing he was, bought Mom slipper socks, because he remembered when he had tubes put in his ears how nurses gave him some and he loved them. Dad tried to tell him that the nurses would give some to Mom, but Ellis wouldn't believe it. Customers talked:

"Why would that man do that to his children?"

"Why didn't he just spank all the little brats?"

"How could he not give in to those little darlings?"

Although I really wanted some food, I'm proud that he didn't give in. Mom wouldn't have either. One hundred dollars is one hundred dollars. The children were testing him big time.

When we arrived home, empty-handed, he had to deal with the millions of messes--the messes that he said would never be if he were home all day. Ha! How he dealt with them was shouting, "Everybody go to your room and don't come out of your room until it's clean."

Violet kept coloring pictures and lining them up, making a beautiful display, but Lilly kept crying, trying to put things where they belonged, throwing all of Violet's art creations in the box that would be thrown out if they weren't put away by the next day. And the boys--they stuffed everything in the closet and under their bed. In fact, they stuffed Lilly underneath their mattress, because she kept whining how Violet wasn't helping. Owen said she'd make a great sandwich.

Speaking of sandwiches, Dad, cooking burgers downstairs (for the third day in a row) heard Lilly's muffled scream, "I can't breathe!" Dad freaked, dropped his spatula and ran upstairs. Dad gave his evil eye to the boys, with that left eyebrow rising an extra inch, lifted the mattress with one hand, and Lilly scurried out.

But then the fire alarm started beeping. Dad freaked again, running downstairs, seeing the burgers burning. Just after he turned off the stove and the alarm, the phone rang. "Did you know your children are out on the roof?" a worried neighbor asked. Dad hung up and ran back upstairs. I chased Dad up and there L.O.V.E. stood in single file on the roof outside the girls' room in the snow. "What the? Get your bodies in here!" he yelled. What are ya trying to do? Kill me?"

"We're just trying not to be killed--like Mommy taught us."

"Yeah, we had a fire drill lots of times."

"We climbed out this window cuz it was far away from the alarm sound."

"Didn't we do the right thing?"

Dad held his head, breathed deeply.

"I need some peace. Everybody go to your room and put dry socks on. Then go downstairs and set the table for dinner."

From my room I heard Dad yell, "Don't I have any socks?" I don't think any of us had matched socks. Nobody had done whites for a week. I didn't answer.

Then, Dad yelled from the bathroom. "What happened to the toilet paper?" Owen hid behind his bedroom door. He had just finished wrapping Violet into a perfect mummy from head to toe—with the last roll of toilet paper. He didn't answer.

"Isn't there any ketchup in this house?" Dad yelled after going downstairs and opening the fridge. Once again, nobody answered. What could we say? His gaze shifted. "How did this jelly get all over this wall?" he yelled again.

This time Ellis chimed in. "Violet wanted to make a pansy garden," he said, putting the plates on the table. Dad filled a coffee cup with day old coffee and stuck it in the microwave. Then he tripped over the apple juice, bean and corn cans that Owen had stacked into a castle. Dad landed against the counter, his grip slipping from the splattering of burger grease.

He fell to the floor, knocking over Owen's army guys ready to attack the castle. We held our breath.

"I don't know how your mother functioned in this tiny kitchen. Everything in this kitchen needs a place. I'm going to make a pantry for her. I can't believe a carpenter's wife doesn't have a pantry. Eat your supper and clean up the dishes and stay out of trouble and listen to Hope." Then, down to the basement he tromped, determined to build a pantry, not to rebuild his heart and soul.

The next morning I kept hearing this banging big time in the basement. Dad had stayed up all night, had built a pantry for Mom--and he was trying to bring it upstairs. The problem was that he built it too big and too well. It stuck between the basement door opening, trapping him in the basement. He yelled obscenities at the "hillbilly shack" we lived in, kicked and pounded the cabinet (as if that would make it shrink half an inch), and then he started body slamming it. Then he stomped back down the stairs and brought up a sledge hammer. He beat on the cabinet. Chips of wood flew off in various angles, but the cabinet didn't budge; it only bruised. "The only problem with making things so well is that they won't fall apart," he said, still stuck in the basement. Then he yowled like a caged, pitiful puppy.

After Aunt Cindy and I finally put the kids down for a nap (I'm thankful she stayed overnight with us and checked on us all of the time), I investigated the cabinet situation. I couldn't budge it, but I squeezed between the top of the door jam and the cabinet and kind of jumped down the stairs.

I saw Dad asleep, stretched out on his workbench, and I saw what looked like X-ray films tacked at eye level along his bench. When I walked closer, I realized they were ultra sound pictures on which Dad had taped little sayings signifying each quad.

"Let's pretend we're astronauts floating in space" aimed at Owen, who had one hand on the umbilical cord.

"Hey, I can't wait to see what beauty awaits me" pointed to Violet.

A foot was the only thing that could be seen of another baby, and the caption read, "Everything better be in order before I come in there." That, I'm sure, was Lilly.

"Can I get anyone anything?" pointed to a hand I assumed was Ellis's.

Then my eyes spied Dad's opened tool box. In it sat a stack of letters that were written on cream-colored stationery. They were all signed *Love, Faith*. They looked so out-of-place--like they didn't belong there in his tool box, and I knew I didn't belong there either. I felt like an intruder, but they stared at me, called to me, enticed me to read them. And I did, because Dad still slept, stretched out on the workbench, even then having jaw muscles clenched. I carefully picked up the first and began to read.

Jacob, I know you want your own business back. I know you're an artist. Please keep in mind that this is only temporary. Don't take other people's attitudes so personally. Detach. Have faith things happen for a reason to teach us what we need. Love, Faith

I took a deep breath and read the next one.

Jacob, I sensed that your dream last night of your dad holding Joshua made you very angry. You seemed angry at God for teasing you, making you think they're still alive. But, you've told me over and over that you really missed them and wanted so much to see them again. Did you ever think the dream was your prayers being answered? God visually told you they were at peace, content. Please surrender your anger, grief. Please quit trying to understand how/why things are as they are. I know you miss Joshua and your father. You know I miss them madly, too. But we have to live in the present. It offers many precious moments that you're missing. Love, Faith.

Who was Joshua? I wondered, but then I saw another letter from Mom. I didn't know if I was ready for this. Already my eyes teared and I feared the truth. But something inside me told me, *Yes, read the letter.*

Jacob, You've beaten yourself up long enough trying to find an answer for why Joshua is no longer with us, why he died at such a young age, why you couldn't help him. Please. Please stop blaming yourself, torturing yourself with what ifs, questioning why things happened as they did, focusing on finding an answer. What happened was not your fault. If I were home and you were working, the same thing could have happened. You must accept the fact that you couldn't have prevented his crib death. It's time to let go of your anger, your grief. God does what he does for reasons we can't understand. Your personal will must be released to divine will if you want to heal. Have faith. You must move on. I want you back into my life. The children and I need you. Love, Faith

Beneath the letter was a white envelope. Inside was the birth certificate of Joshua Jacob Johnson. My jaw dropped. I had another brother. The guilt I felt for invading Mom and Dad's privacy settled over me like sawdust. Feeling vulnerable, naked in the brightness, I turned off the light, hoping to escape like a robber in the night. But in the darkness, I could finally see the light. Everything made sense now. I had another brother who had died from crib death. From looking at his birth certificate, he was born on Dad's birthday, exactly eleven months after I was born. No wonder Dad hated his birthday. He felt responsible, because Joshua died when Dad was home and Mom was working at the hospital. After Joshua died, Dad became closer than ever with his father. His father helped him through his grief, I suppose, because when I was little we had a lot of fun together. But the day Mom had the quads, Grandpa died, devastating Dad again. He didn't want to get close, thinking he'd just be hurt again. Plus, he couldn't take the turmoil. Too many changes too fast.

I felt like my body was turning into ice. I started shaking, sobbing, feeling numb like a frozen tundra. Then I spied the marble jar on Dad's workbench, and I remembered how holding those marbles gave me warmth when I was younger, because I'd hold the marbles and then Dad's huge hands covered mine. I used to imagine the pink peeries glowing right through my hands, penetrating pink light through his, too. And I remembered how he'd rub my hands and I'd feel the marbles massaging my palms. Then he'd say, "Make a wish," and after I would, he'd direct my hands over the marble jar and opened my fingers slightly and the marbles would all tinkle back into the jar.

I poured some marbles into my hands, closed my eyes, and began rubbing the marbles, wishing--praying for my father to come back to me, come back to himself, find his spirit. My hands began to feel so warm, as an egg would beneath a mother bird, as a child would, wrapped by an angel's wings.

When I opened my eyes, the dark basement filled with light and the only thing in sight was the blue-eyed angel, whose hands covered mine. Then, I watched a prism of light permeate from my hands and penetrate into the ultra sound picture of L.O.V.E. From there it flowed, pouring into Dad's chest. His entire body glowed, and then Dad awoke; he stared, wide-eyed, as the angel spoke in a sweet whisper:

"Joshua, your little angel,
lives now with the angels.
His heart beats
to the beat of his wings
and your love."

Silence permeated the room. Then she spoke again, still looking at Dad.

"Your father, son and brother
live in land, sea and sky.
Find them everywhere—
With your heart, ears and eyes."

In silence, the angel wrapped us with her wings, warmed us through, cracked our fears into useless shells. She kissed me on the top of my head and guided my hands to the marble jar. She then became colors, a rainbow, which arched from Dad's chest through the ultrasound pictures to my hands still holding the marbles. Then a pretty, yellow sticky note fluttered out of nowhere, and like a little yellow butterfly, landed at our feet.

Forgive yourself and others.
Yes, forgiveness is the key
that opens up our hearts
to be happy, light and free.

My jaw dropped and my fingers slightly parted and the marbles tinkled back into the jar, pulling the prism of light with them. All fear left me and I felt peaceful, and hopeful, as I would when watching the yawning and stretching out of a new dawn, a new day.

The next thing I remember was Dad kind of shaking me, waking me up, picking me up off of the basement floor.

"Hey, how'd you get down here and why are you on the cold floor?"

"Oh, Dad," I said confused, looking around, hoping to find the beautiful rainbow of light. "What a dream I had!"

"You, too?" he asked, lifting me to my feet. And then as if nothing happened, we climbed the stairs and

Dad helped me climb up over the pantry cabinet, so I could reach the other side. He tossed me over a screwdriver and guided me and Aunt Cindy in how to unscrew the screws and move the basement door off of its hinges. Now when Dad pushed on the cabinet, it glided through the opening.

Still on his knees on the steps, he stayed perfectly still for a minute, and then he crawled up the last two stairs. His head poked into the kitchen; his eyes squinted. He stood up slowly, stretching, and he walked tentatively into the light. Then he hugged me, darn near smothered me. I savored the moment, witnessing the once tightly wound cocoon changing, finally, into a fragile, yet freed butterfly. But in my mind I feared the inevitable, that everything that had just happened was only a dream and Dad would walk into a spider's web he'd woven himself. Well, I was right. Change was inevitable.

Dad had truly metamorphosed. He no longer inched along in his self-pity. He flew. Shhheeeww. He looked around the house, a scary sight. Then he gathered all of the kids in the kitchen, huddled them up, including me and said, "Before your mother comes home, there will be a place for everything and everything in its place." The children moaned. Dad had disappeared into the basement for a day and the minute he had them all together, his only concern was a clean house. They all moaned, speaking aloud their thoughts.

"Ah, Dad. Do we have to clean again?" and "I miss Mommy. When is she coming home?" and "When are we going to have our stuffed animal parade?" and "Can't we just play somewhere without being yelled at that we're making a mess?" were all questions rapidly fired at Dad. Dad just stood there, actually listening, and then his metamorphosis became visible to everyone. Instead of pointing, directing, yelling, he quietly asked the following question, while raising his arms up into a V shape, palms up: "How hard can it be to put all of your toys in one room, in the play room?" We all looked confused. "Dad, we don't have a play room, I said."

"Come with me," he said.

Dad methodically walked to the locked, forbidden door, the door he told us went nowhere. Next to the door squatted a little stand. On the stand sat an old Bible. Within the Bible's pages lay a gold key. Dad picked up the key, and paused, it seemed like forever, before fitting the key inside the lock and turning it. He pushed gently on the door and then poked his head in, breathing deeply, before fully entering the room. Inside, a baby nursery containing bright, primary colored walls displaying tons of framed photographs welcomed us and our jaws dropped in awe when we eyed the beautifully crafted wooden carousel with four horses in the middle of the room.

"Wow!" "Cool!" "Awesome!" and "Yippy-Yaw-Hoo!" exploded from the children as they ran inside, unable to stop themselves. Dad allowed us to explore for a few minutes and then called us to him. He got down on one knee, huddling us around him. "Children, I locked this room a long time ago, only coming back in when I installed the horse carousel that I built for you."

"That's ours?" shouted Violet.

"It sure is. I'm sorry I didn't show it to you 'til now. I thought if I kept things just as they were I would be able to hold on to the past, thinking that was the best thing to do. But with your help and the help from my angel, I'm learning to let go and..." he paused, not really knowing what to say.

"Let God?" answered Ellis.

"Yes, that's it. Have faith that things happen for a reason. Forgive myself for things and forgive others, and..." Dad bit his lip, turned his face from us so we couldn't see the tears. Owen broke the awkwardness. "Dad, is this you?" He pointed to the black and white photo.

"No, that's my Dad, your Grandpa Joshua."

"Wow. We had a Grandpa Joshua?"

"Yes. My father was your Grandpa Joshua that you never met.

He passed away the day you were born."

"This one is Daddy," said Owen. "Look, he's holding a baseball bat."

"No, that's your Uncle Joshua. Uncle Joshua was my older brother. You never got to meet him either." (I learned later that he was killed with a baseball, and that's why Dad never let me play ball. I thought it was because I was a girl).

"This one looks like Daddy when he was a baby."

"No, that is your brother, Joshua, your brother who..."

"Lives with the angels," I answered for him. When my Dad turned to me, his knowing eyes told me that the angel dream wasn't a dream and he had experienced it, too.

"We have another brother?" asked Ellis.

"Yes, well, uh, no. Eleven months after Hope was born and eleven years before you kids were born, you had another brother. This room was his. I locked it up after he died. I didn't want anything to change; I wanted to try and keep things the same. But then my father helped me realize there's still a beautiful life, despite sadness. You see he too had lost a son, but he learned to move on, and he helped me move on, helped me love life again. He even helped me and your mother name you kids. But the day you were born, he died suddenly, his heart stopped, and I became really angry—angry that you'd never know him—and I became really afraid to grow close to you because I didn't want to be hurt again. I'm sorry that I was scared to show my love for you. I'm sorry that I hid myself so well from you that I couldn't be found."

I don't know how much of what my dad said the quads actually grasped, but Owen responded with, "Well, geeze, Dad. If I knew you were playing hide-n-go-seek, I would have tapped you to be 'It.'"

"And it would have been easy because you were always hiding out in the basement," said Violet.

Dad smiled. "Well, I was not only hiding out, but I was lost. Lost in the past, lost in anger, lost in grief. I couldn't forgive myself, God, the world—for what happened to my brother, my son, my father, but I was seeking the wrong things."

"What were you looking for" asked Lilly.

"I was looking for the answers to why things happened as they did. I wanted to find the answer out *there* somewhere," he said, pointing out the window. What I've learned is that some things I'll never know—some things will always be a mystery. And

42

that's Okay. I'll have to trust in God that they happened for a reason. I nearly drove myself crazy looking for the reason, and I know I drove your poor mother crazy looking for the reason."

"Hope always says, 'Peace, be still,' when we drive her crazy," said Lilly.

"Your sister is really something. What good advice—be still long enough to find the peaceful place inside, the happiness within. Too many people, including myself, search everywhere else but inside. Well, I'm done being angry now. I know I have to stop focusing on the past and live in the moment."

"Wow. The Kitchen Fairy finally got through to you, huh?" questioned Ellis.

Dad smiled. "Yes, she certainly did. She's an angel." Dad pulled us all in close to him. You children are all gifts to me, yourself, and the world."

"Speaking of gifts, look at this," I said, handing him a present wrapped in a comic strip section of the newspaper. It had a tag that read:

To Dad with love from Faith, Hope and L.O.V.E.

"Oh, my gosh. It's the Joshua picture. Your mom gave this to me when you kids came home from the hospital. After I opened it, though, I stuck it right back in the box, thinking since they had all died that I shouldn't be reminded of them." Dad picked up the picture frame out of the box and pointed out each photo in the frame. "This is your Grandpa Joshua; my brother, Joshua; and your baby brother, Joshua."

"Wow. That's cool that they were all named Joshua," I whispered, looking at each picture up close.

"My mom told me once that Joshua was a great leader. Although these three Joshua's aren't here today, I believe they are still leading me, teaching me. I can't guarantee that I can change overnight, but I'm sure going to look at things differently and try my best," said Dad.

"Mom always said to try and see things out of a different person's glasses," said Owen.

"I have a baby skunk named Joshua," said Lilly. Everyone laughed.

When Dad picked up the box that contained the frame, he realized that there was something else in it. It, too, was wrapped in comics and had a tag:

To Dad with love from Faith, Hope and L.O.V.E.

Inside was a frame with a baby picture of all of us kids and mom. The following words were written on a red, heart-shaped sticky note.

> Anything can be accomplished with
> Faith, Hope and Love. Keep smiling!
>
> --Love and hugs, The Kitchen Fairy

Everyone cheered. "Yeah!" and "We're awesome!" and "We're a great team, just like Mom said!" and "The Kitchen Fairy is soooo cool!" I saw dad wiping some tears again and I found myself pinching myself. I wasn't sure if I was dreaming or not.

"Well, gather all of the toys from everywhere around the house and bring them here. You all now have a play room," said Dad.

Once again we all cheered. We organized the room throughout the day while Dad organized the new pantry in the kitchen. Then we all sat down for lunch. When Lilly had a melt down because there were water spots on her glass, Dad amazed me by swapping glasses with her and then showing her how easy the spots could be wiped off with his handkerchief. When Owen said, "Daddy, can you pretend you're Tyrannosaurus Rex and I'm a raptor?" Dad immediately drew in his elbows to his sides and pinched his fingers together and chased him around the table, sending him reeling through the house laughing, instead of saying, "Why do you think we had so many kids? Go play with one of them and stay out of my hair!" When Ellis said, "Dad, there's something really cool I have to show you," Dad checked out the huge spider web in the corner of the playroom instead of saying, "I'm busy now." When Violet wanted some paper to draw with, Dad didn't give her another lecture on how she wrecked his plans and should stay out of people's stuff, but instead he brought up a box of sawdust from the basement and drew a flower with glue on some scrap wood and sprinkled it with the sawdust he called "fairy dust" and told her to create something of her own on the other pieces. Then he gave everyone a piece of scrap wood and told us to decorate it anyhow we wanted to with paint, markers, glitter, or "fairy dust." Then he told the quads and me to pick out our favorite place in the room so he could hang up our wooden design, designating our own special space in the playroom. We had a blast.

When Owen asked Dad what happened to make him be so different, Dad said he had a sudden change of heart. When Lilly asked him what made his heart change, he said he met an angel. When Ellis asked if Mom was the angel he said she was definitely an angel but didn't think she was *the* angel. When Violet asked if the angel was the Kitchen Fairy he said he knew the Kitchen Fairy was an *angel* but didn't know if they were one and the same. When I asked if Mom was the Kitchen Fairy, he said we would have to ask her, because he wasn't sure anymore—or ever.

By this time, everybody was pooped out. Aunt Cindy came over to help put the quads to bed so Dad could go and visit Mom again. Before he left, however, he took me by the hand and led me to the basement. He pulled out another ultra sound picture from a bin and pointed to a note taped on it in his own handwriting. It read:

"Daddy's little joy doesn't have to be a boy."

I had never seen my own ultrasound picture before (maybe because I was in such a "it's definitely a girl" position). Dad hung it from the workbench along with the others. "I know you thought I was disappointed that you were a girl, but I'm not. You have been a wonderful daughter, Hope. I'm so proud of you and thankful that you are in my world." Then he hugged me tightly. I felt such calming energy, like a warm light filling me up, lifting up my heart and calming my soul.

During Dad's visit with Mom that night, Mom made incredible improvement. While holding Dad's hand, Mom said she could feel this warm energy surging through her, energizing her, and she felt strong enough to come home. The doctors were amazed what progress she had made, just three days ago being so weak from mere exhaustion and disoriented with a slight concussion. (At first the doctors thought she had heart troubles because Dad said he had done CPR because he couldn't feel her pulse. Fortunately, the doctors determined that her heart was fine and that the reason he couldn't feel her pulse was because it was so weak and he was so scared). In any case, everyone agreed that she could leave in the morning, as long as she would have plenty of help at home to recover.

Her eyes grew like balloons when Dad and I and the quads flocked into her hospital room the next morning to bring her home. L.O.V.E. surrounded her, handing her pictures, painted rocks, stuffed animals and an angel watch. She cried with joy and even the doctor's eyes teared up. The only problem was that her big olive eyes turned to Dad and me and she asked, "Who are all of these loving children?"

Trouble there.

Tam e. Polzer

Part Three: Thirty Years Later

L.O.V.E. have their own loves now. Lilly is a curator of a history museum and loves how everything is in its place. She is married to a surgeon. Owen is a Green Beret. His specialty is paratrooping. When he's away, his wife has trouble keeping their twin sons off of the roof. Violet has around one hundred children every year—she is an elementary art teacher and is married to a man who owns his own photography business. Ellis is a psychologist and was recently on a talk show for his research in therapeutic touch. Dad works full-time now in the basement making dollhouses, airplanes and wooden horses and plays a lot of marbles with the grandkids. Mom works part-time as a home-care nurse and babysits the grandkids now and then. Me? I'm a freelance writer and married to a carpenter. We have an awesome son and daughter, three cats and two dogs, six tractors and a farm and live in the snow belt in Northeastern Ohio.

I'm so thankful that all of us have found loving mates, have healthy children, and are doing what makes us happy. I'm also thankful for video cameras and photographs—with them it didn't take long for Mom to remember that she, indeed, was the mother of quadruplets. The only things she still doesn't remember are writing the Kitchen Fairy notes or the night she collapsed. What I'm most grateful for, however, are the Angel and the Kitchen Fairy. They taught the kids some life lessons, they pulled my dad out of the darkness, they showed me that miracles can happen every day, and they reminded us all what's really important after all:

When we think we've lost everything and can't find any joy, we must break through illusion and remember,

"There are three things that remain--faith, hope and love-- and the greatest of these is love."

1 Corinthians 13

ABOUT THE AUTHOR

Tam e. Polzer, a retired high school English teacher, enjoys writing everything from silly children's poetry to serious essays. She loves taking walks, riding her bike, doing yoga, playing live music with her friends in the barn her husband built, conducting up-lifting workshops, creating gifts of poetry enhanced with pressed flowers and leaves for her business called Nature's Way, helping her husband maintain their property and huge vegetable garden, and spending time with family, friends and her adult children. Her favorite expression is "Keep smiling."

Feel free to visit her business page at www.facebook.com/natureswaybyte to see her pressed flowers/leaves preserved with verse for all occasions and other links to her writing.

24443729R00036

Made in the USA
San Bernardino, CA
24 September 2015